J Harrin
Harrington, Claudia
Otis the very large dog

$27.07
ocn958781835

Hank the Pet Sitter

#1

Otis the Very Large Dog

by Claudia Harrington   illustrated by Anoosha Syed

Calico Kid

An Imprint of Magic Wagon
abdopublishing.com

In loving memory of Gus, the first best big dog.
And Gulliver, who loved laps —CH

For Mama and Papa —AS

abdopublishing.com

Published by Magic Wagon, a division of ABDO, PO Box 398166, Minneapolis, Minnesota 55439. Copyright © 2017 by Abdo Consulting Group, Inc. International copyrights reserved in all countries. No part of this book may be reproduced in any form without written permission from the publisher. Calico Kid™ is a trademark and logo of Magic Wagon.

Printed in the United States of America, North Mankato, Minnesota.
092016
012017

Written by Claudia Harrington
Illustrated by Anoosha Syed
Edited by Heidi M.D. Elston
Art Directed by Candice Keimig

Publisher's Cataloging in Publication Data

Names: Harrington, Claudia, author. I Syed, Anoosha, illustrator.
Title: Otis the very large dog / by Claudia Harrington ; illustrated by Anoosha Syed.
Description: Minneapolis, MN : Magic Wagon, 2017. I Series: Hank the pet sitter ; Book 1
Summary: Hank pet sits Otis the very large dog. Otis gets a toothache, and Hank has to take him to the vet.
Identifiers: LCCN 2016947637 I ISBN 9781624021879 (lib. bdg.) I ISBN 9781624022470 (ebook) I ISBN 9781624022777 (Read-to-me ebook)
Subjects: LCSH: Dogs–Juvenile fiction. I Pet sitting–Juvenile fiction. I Pets–Juvenile fiction.
Classification: DDC [E]–dc23
LC record available at http://lccn.loc.gov/2016947637

Table of Contents

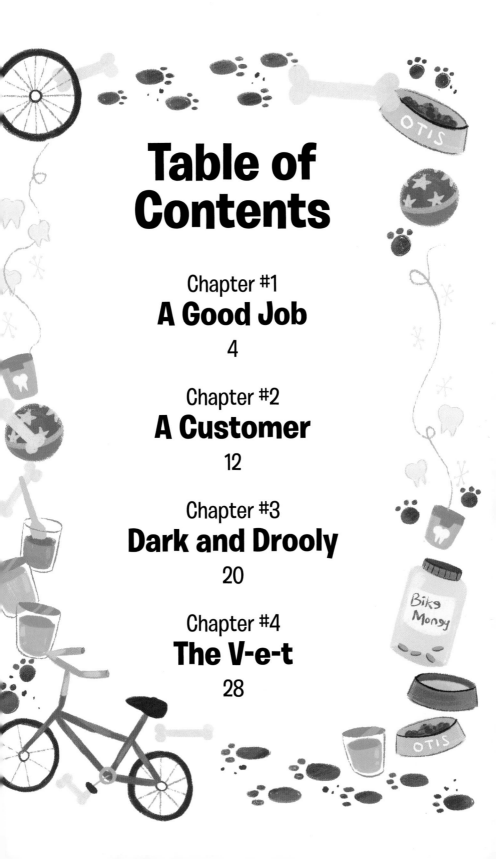

Chapter #1
A Good Job

It was the first day of summer. Hank loved summer. He loved swimming in the pond. He loved playing ball with his friends.

5

But most of all, Hank loved riding his bike.

"My bike!" yelled Hank. He looked at the bent metal. It looked like modern art.

"You need to put away your things," said Hank's mom.

"You need to pay for a new bike," said Hank's dad.

"But I'm a kid!" said Hank.

Janie ran over from next door. "Tsk," she said.

Hank hated when she clicked her tongue like that.

"Why don't you mow lawns?" asked Janie.

Hank shook his head.

"Why don't you weed?" asked Janie. She pulled a small shovel out of her purse.

Hank shook his head again.

"Hey, Mom! Hey, Dad!" said Hank. "Can I pet sit?"

Hank's mom looked at Hank's dad. They smiled.

"I need a sign!" said Hank.

Hank got to work. He got a poster board from the closet. He got the old cans of red and orange paint from the garage.

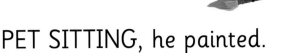

PET SITTING, he painted.

ALL KINDS, he painted.

HANK, he painted. But he messed up the *a*, and it looked like an *o*.

Still, it was a good sign. Hank was ready for business!

Chapter #2
A Customer

Hank stood on the lawn with his sign. A car drove by and honked. Hank waved.

"What are you doing?" asked Janie.

"Waving," said Hank. "They might be customers."

"Tsk," Janie clicked again. "They are not customers."

"But they honked," said Hank.

Janie tugged on gloves from her purse. She pointed to the sign. "Your sign says *honk*."

PeTSitting
ALL KiNDS
Honk

"Why don't you go home?" asked Hank. "You aren't good for business."

Hank's friend Ben and his mom pulled up. Ben's mom honked.

Their car was stuffed with suitcases. It was stuffed with Ben. But mostly, it was stuffed with Ben's huge dog, Otis.

HONK!

"Can you pet sit Otis?" asked Ben's mom. "If not, we will take him to the vet."

Vet!

Otis jumped. He hit his big head on the roof of the car.

"Mom," said Ben, "you have to spell that word."

"Sorry," said Ben's mom. "Hank? Is it okay? We have to go."

"Sure," said Hank. He had his first customer!

Ben lugged a giant bin of food from the car. He lugged a giant bed from the car. Finally, he lugged his giant dog, Otis, from the car.

Hank grabbed Otis's leash. "Hi, boy!" he said.

Ben's mom waved as Ben got in the car. "Thanks, Hank. Otis hates the vet!"

Vet!

But Hank didn't hear her. He was too busy holding on for dear life.

Chapter #3
Dark and Drooly

"Dinner, Otis!" called Hank.

Otis slid to the floor.

"You have to eat," said Hank.

"Watch!"

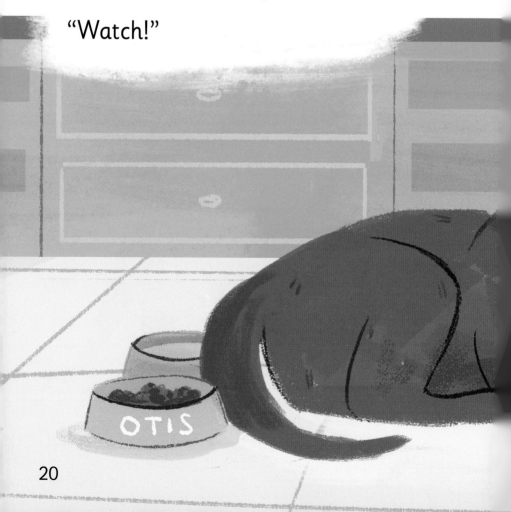

Hank tasted some kibble. "Yuck!"

"He misses Ben," said Hank's mom. "He'll adjust."

Otis didn't adjust after dinner. He didn't adjust by bedtime.

He didn't even adjust by morning.

"Come on out, Otis!" said Hank. "I can't lose my first customer."

"You got a customer!" said Janie.

"Don't your parents ever miss you?" asked Hank.

"What's he doing in your tree?" asked Janie.

"He needs time to adjust," said Hank.

Janie pulled out doctor stuff. "Did you take his temperature?"

"He's not sick," said Hank.

Otis groaned.

"Watch!" said Hank. He got five flavors of Jell-O.

Otis stuck his head out, then hid again.

"Maybe he *is* sick," said Hank.

Janie put on a mask. She handed Hank a flashlight. "Check his throat."

Hank peered in.

"What do you see?" asked Janie.

"Smelly dark. Covered in drool."

"Let me see," said Janie. "His tooth! It's black at the bottom."

"They all are," said Hank.

"Well, I think it should come out," said Janie. "Do you have any string?"

Ben would blame Hank for that tooth. His business would be ruined. Hank would never get his new bike.

"I'll get the string," said Hank.

When Hank left, Janie sat down. Otis saw her lap and leaped.

"Ahhhhh!" yelled Janie.

Arooooo! howled Otis.

Hank skidded in. "What did you do?" he asked.

"Get him off me!" said Janie.

"Don't move," said Hank. "I have dental floss. It's mint."

"Hurry," said Janie. "I can't breathe."

Chapter #4
The V-e-t

"What are you up to?" asked Hank's mom.

"It's his tooth. Can I use the pliers?" asked Hank.

"Hello," said Janie. "Can't breathe."

"Time for the vet," said Hank's mom.

Vet!

Otis ran behind the plant.

"Thanks, Mom," said Hank.

The v-e-t checked Otis. "His tooth has to come out."

"Out?" asked Hank.

"Out," said the vet. "It's cracked. But don't worry. Otis won't feel anything."

Otis was groggy when he came out.
Hank and Janie pulled him home,
huffing and puffing.

"Sure you don't want to mow
lawns?" asked Janie.

When they got home, Hank said,
"Out, Otis."

Otis snored.

"Come, Otis," said Janie.

Otis drooled.

Hank ran inside for Jell-O. Otis opened his eyes and ate the Jell-O. Every last wiggle.

Then Otis gave Hank the slobberiest kiss ever. Pet sitting was going to be okay.